Fudgesicle

Tinée Furbert

Illustrated by: Gherdai Hassell

To Skyla and Brazil for
inspiring me to always be
my best self.

Love, Mommy

In honor of all the special ladies in my life, you know who you are! Mom, Camille, Mikeema, Derricka, Anya, Noey, Allana, Simone, GiGi and my beloved Keita Wilson, I love and miss you.

-TF

Fudgesicle

"Hey Novi, have you ever had a fudgesicle?
Novi smiled, "No Mommy, but it sounds yummy!"

“Just like you, it’s a smooth **CHESTNUT** dynamic delight.” Novi’s mom said.
“I’m going to take you to get one.”

"Fudgesicles come in many flavors."
"What do you think they are?"

There's chestnut, cinnamon, cocoa, molasses, mocha, chocolate, and caramel.

"I can't wait to taste fudgesicles, SO many choices. Let's see!," Novi said.

"**Cinnamon** looks like YOU Mommy!" Novi explained, excitedly.

"A heavenly-made, valued, dainty delight."

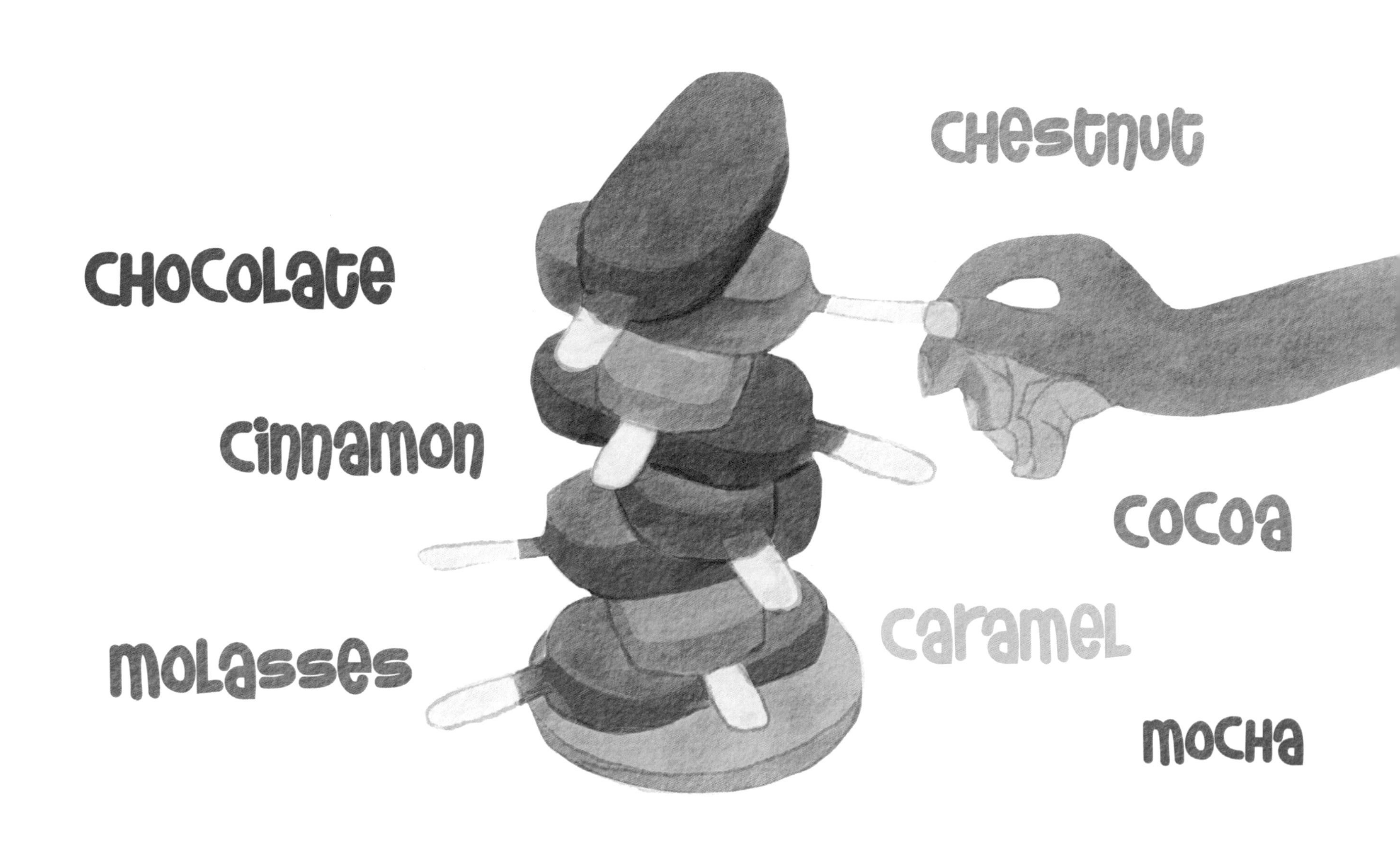

"The **molasses** fudgesicle looks like my friend Ava."

"A phenomenal, awe-inspiring, dreamy delight."

"There's **cocoa** like you know who . . . Nana."

"A sensational yummy, dandy delight."

"There's **MOCHA** like Daddy."

"A frosty, one of a kind definite delight."

"Do you think **chocolate** looks like Godma Kee?" Novi asked.

"Of course! A wondrous, awesome, divine delight," Mommy replied.

Novi said, "And last but not least, there's **caramel**, like Aunt Millie."

"A unique, remarkable, delicious delight."

"So Novi, which fudgesicle do you want?" Mommy asked.

"I can't make up my mind, they all look delicious," said Novi.

"Should I choose **CHESTNUT** that looks like me or **MOCHA** that looks like Daddy?"

"Alright, I choose **CHESTNUT** that looks like me!"

Thank you Mommy for the fudgesicle!

You're welcome, my beautiful brown girl," Mommy said.

"MOMMIEEE!
I dropped my **CHESTNUT** fudgesicle," Novi sobbed.

Novi's Mom said, "It's OK
Novi, look up with
confidence and smile."

"I'm thinking about that fudgy filled place
we just came from."

Novi asked,

"Could we go back?"

"Let's go buy another . . ."

"Dynamic Dainty"

"Dreamy Dandy"

"Definitely Divine"

"Chestnut fudgesicle delight ...Like Me!"

Color me !

About the Author

Tinee Furbert is a Bermudian author and occupational therapist. She has a passion for children's literature. Tinee remembers as a child calling into Bermuda Youth Library's "Dial-A-Story" to listen to bedtime stories every night. It was only fitting that she would set out on the journey of writing a children's book. Tinee recognizes the power of storytelling to empower black and brown girls and women to be their best and whole selves. When she is not advocating for young exceptional people and seniors, she enjoys traveling, food tasting and spending time with loved ones. She lives and works in Bermuda with her family and her fur baby, Remy Ma.

About the Illustrator

Gherdai Hassell is a Bermudian contemporary artist, illustrator and storyteller. She is the winner of the Best of Bermuda Artist Award 2021 and 2022. She earned her MFA at the China Academy of Art and is a member of Delta Sigma Theta Sorority, Inc. Her works can be found in private and public collections across the world. When she is not in her studio making artwork, she enjoys spending time with family and friends, her pets, traveling, and reading. She lives and works in Manchester, UK.

Fudgesicle

ISBN: 978-0-947482-12-1 (Hardcover)
ISBN: 978-0-947482-15-2 (Paperback)
ISBN: 978-0-947482-16-9 (eBook)

Library of Congress Control Number: Pending

Editorial Advisor: Janet Squires

Illustrations: Gherdai Hassell

Formatting: Juan Roberts

Literary Director: Sandra Slayton James

Lightning Source UK Ltd.
Milton Keynes UK
UKRC030821240123
415817UK00001B/4